Gonzalo Grabs the Good Life

Written by **Janice Levy**

Illustrated by **Bill Slavin**

Eerdmans Books for Young Readers

Grand Rapids, Michigan ✳ Cambridge, U.K.

After Gonzalo won the lottery, he hopped off
the roof and pecked don Chucho on the nose.

"I'm rich!" he said. "Get another rooster. I quit!"

"But Gonzalo," the farmer said. "Aren't you happy here?"

Gonzalo fluffed his feathers. "I don't like to complain,
but the hens cluck all night, and the horse snores.
The roof is so hard that my back hurts.
I haven't slept in a week."

Gonzalo packed his bags. "*Adiós*, don Chucho.
This rooster stuff is nothing to crow about.
It's time to grab the good life!"

And off he went.

His feathers fell out in the hot tub.

His beak got stuck in the putting green.

"*¡Ay, caramba!*" Gonzalo said. "This is not the good life."

Gonzalo became a party animal.

He went out to Hollywood
and lived *la vida loca*.

He stayed up all night eating candy.

But Gonzalo got fat.

His feet hurt from dancing.

He was too tired to cock-a-doodle-doo.

Soon he ran out of money.
Then he ran out of friends.

Nobody wanted a poor guy in feathers
who used to sing for his supper.

"*¡Ay, caramba!*" Gonzalo said. "This is
not the good life."

Gonzalo went to church and prayed.

He sang and swayed.

Padre Juan asked him to sing in the choir.

Word spread about the singing rooster. His solos were the talk of the town. The church was packed every Sunday.

But still Gonzalo wasn't happy.

"I don't like to complain, but the ducks quack off-key, the frogs won't sit still, and the owls don't give a hoot. The hummingbirds forget the words. The pigeons are pooping everywhere!"

Gonzalo's beak drooped. "*¡Ay, caramba!* This is not the good life."

Padre Juan rubbed his chin. "A wise man once said, 'When you can't find your car keys, they're usually in your pocket.'"

That night, Gonzalo had a strange dream. Don Chucho wore ruby red sneakers and danced to reggaeton music on a rooftop. The hens ran away with Padre Juan's car keys. A tornado blew everything across the sky.

"Gonzalo, go home," the wind whispered.
"*Adiós*, Gonzalo . . . Gonzalo, go home."

"Fine," said don Chucho. "I've got my own problems. Look on the roof. The mouse overslept."

"The mouse crows?"

"Crows shmows," don Chucho said. "I'm lucky if he gives a little squeak."

Don Chucho snapped his fingers. "Gonzalo, can you still sing?"

The rooster fluffed his feathers. "Does the sun still rise?"

From that morning on,
Gonzalo danced across the roof and . . .

CROWED!

He even stopped complaining —
most of the time.

Vocabulario: Vocabulary

adiós: good-bye

don: Mister (Mr.)

¡Ay, caramba!: oh, dear!

la vida loca: the crazy life

Padre: Father

reggaeton: Hispanic hip-hop music

To Rick, with all my love
— J.L.

For Evelyn and all her crazy chickens
— B.S.

Text © Janice Levy
Illustrations © Bill Slavin

Published in 2009 by Eerdmans Books for Young Readers
an imprint of Wm. B. Eerdmans Publishing Co.

Wm. B. Eerdmans Publishing Co.
2140 Oak Industrial Dr. NE, Grand Rapids, Michigan 49505
P.O. Box 163, Cambridge CB3 9PU U.K.

www.eerdmans.com/youngreaders

Manufactured in China

16 15 14 13 12 11 10 09   9 8 7 6 5 4 3 2 1

Library of Congress Cataloging-in-Publication Data

Levy, Janice.
Gonzalo grabs the good life / by Janice Levy; illustrated by Bill Slavin.
p. cm.
Summary: When Gonzalo the rooster wins the lottery, he leaves his job
at the farm in search of the good life.

ISBN 978-0-8028-5328-8 (alk. paper)

[1. Wealth — Fiction. 2. Roosters — Fiction.] I. Slavin, Bill, ill. II. Title.
PZ7.L5832Go 2009
[E] — dc22
2008009998

Display and text type set in Impress BT
Illustrations created with acrylics on gessoed paper
Illustrations by Bill Slavin with Esperança Melo